GUINEA PIG

PET SHOP PRIVATE EYE

#6

Going, Going, Dragon!

BAD BREATH!

COLLEEN AF VENABLE   ILLUSTRATED BY STEPHANIE YUE

GRAPHIC UNIVERSE

GUINEA PIG

PET SHOP PRIVATE EYE

#6

Going, Going, Dragon!

COLLEEN AF VENABLE

ILLUSTRATED BY STEPHANIE YUE

GRAPHIC UNIVERSE™ · MINNEAPOLIS

Story by Colleen AF Venable

Art by Stephanie Yue

Coloring by Hi-Fi Design

Lettering by Grace Lu

Copyright © 2013 by Lerner Publishing Group, Inc.

Graphic Universe™ is a trademark of Lerner Publishing Group, Inc.

Graphic Universe™
A division of Lerner Publishing Group, Inc.
241 First Avenue North
Minneapolis, MN 55401 USA

For reading levels and more information, look up this title at www.lernerbooks.com.

Library of Congress Cataloging-in-Publication Data

Venable, Colleen AF.
    Going, going, dragon! / by Colleen AF Venable ; illustrated by Stephanie Yue.
        p.   cm. — (Guinea PIG, pet shop private eye ; #06)
    Summary: Sasspants, Hamisher, and company have never been so raucous at the Mr. Venezi's Pets and Stuff pet supplies shop. This time, there's scuba diving in the fish tank with the Steves, what appears to be a dragon hiding behind the counter, and Mr. Venezi's insistence that the store has been robbed of $1,000.
        ISBN 978-0-7613-6009-4 (lib. bdg. : alk. paper)
        ISBN 978-1-4677-0973-6 (eBook)
    1. Graphic novels. [1. Graphic novels. 2. Mystery and detective stories. 3. Pet shops—Fiction. 4. Guinea pigs—Fiction. 5. Hamsters—Fiction. 6. Dragons—Fiction. 7. Animals—Fiction. 8. Humorous stories.] I. Yue, Stephanie, illustrator. II. Title.
PZ7.7.V46Go 2013
741.5'973—dc23   2012047641

Manufactured in the United States of America
2 – HF – 11/1/14

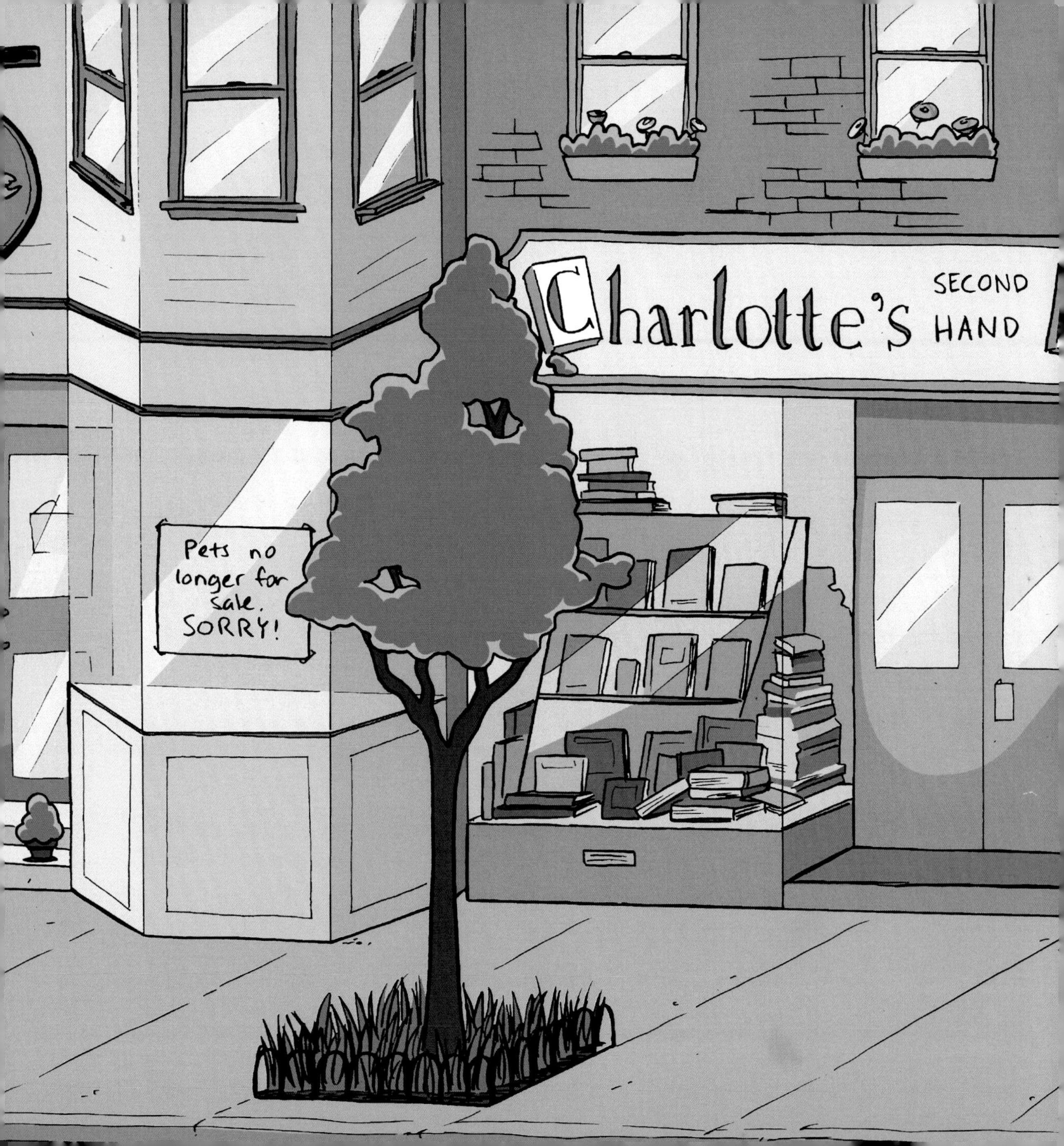
Charlotte's SECOND HAND
Pets no longer for sale. SORRY!

Hello and welcome to Mr. Venezi's and Stuff. We don't sell pets anymore!

Sign here.

No problem! I have a pen right...

My pen! It's gone!

A mystery!

A mystery?

A MYSTERY?!

A mys-- --tery!

A missed tree?

I MISS IT SO MUCH!

Hey! I found the tree!

I MISSED YOU SO MUCH, TREE!

It's a good thing this pet shop has its own detectives!

Yeah!

This looks like a job for...

...Detectives Sasspants and Hamisher?

I keep telling you guys. We aren't detectives! Not anymore.

Mmmmmuh muuuuh muh muuuuh...

We retired.

I just said that!

Now we're deep-sea explorers! The astronauts of the ocean! Check out my awesome ocean astronaut helmet! I ordered it online!

Oof! Is this a paperweight?

Yup!

But what about Mr. Venezi's missing pen?!

WAHH!

I'm sure he'll find it when he tries to put another pen behind his ear.

CLANK

There's a pen be--

Viola! Thank goodness you're here. There's been a robbery!

bing bong!

A robbery?

Someone stole my pen! I'm not sure who or why. But we're going to figure it out! First, we have to think: who has a motive? My guess is that Shakespeare guy. Didn't he write something? Where did he get the pen?!

PLUCK!

Great job, assistant! You should get a commissioner for that! Shakespeare was smart to hide it there! My eyes can't turn that way.

7

Walrus toothbrushes? Mr. V, how many times do I have to tell you? We don't have walruses in the shop!

I know. I figured since we weren't selling pets anymore, I should have a bigger variety of supplies to make up for it. Now everyone in town who owns a walrus will come to Mr. Venezi's and Stuff!

How are the tortillas?

You're close, but that's not what they are called.

I meant the tortillas at Gas-o Taco. I know all about your double chinchillas.

I don't have a double chin!

I think he means "two chinchillas."

Nice, Mr. V! You're really learning the animals' names.

I want Charlotte to think I'm smart. I want her to take me seriously.

Now, help me find a good spot for these walrus toothbrushes. I have to make room for a box of aardvark neckties that's arriving tomorrow.

I'm getting worried Mr. V's spending too much money. The pet shop isn't exactly bringing in a lot of income lately.

MMmmmmmm mmmmmmm mmmm . . .

...and think of how big walrus breath mints would have to be!

I can't hear you at all when you have this helmet on. And it's so heavy. Are you sure you don't want me to make you a snorkel like mine?

No way! I'm an ocean astronaut and I look super cool. Follow my lead! I've been swimming before. I'll teach you! Just be REALLY careful you don't...

...mmmm ammmm mmmm!

SPLASH!

EEP!

Another missed tree!

Is that how swimming works?

Yeah, he totally missed the tree!

We've been doing it wrong!

THUNK

Why are you frowning, Steve?

I'm not frowning. Why are YOU frowning, Steve?

Stop laughing.

I'm not laughing.

Hey, Sasspants! What are you guys today?

Definitely NOT ocean astronauts.

We're still deciding what we want to be.

I don't know why you don't want to be detectives anymore. You were so great at it!

Don't encourage them.

SHAKE SHAKE SHAKE

You guys are doing fine without us. Besides, you have a new shop detective!

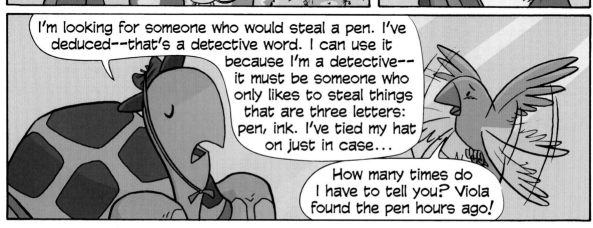

I'm looking for someone who would steal a pen. I've deduced--that's a detective word. I can use it because I'm a detective-- it must be someone who only likes to steal things that are three letters: pen, ink. I've tied my hat on just in case...

How many times do I have to tell you? Viola found the pen hours ago!

How is it living with Viola?

We love it.

She made us these supersoft beds, and every night she sings to us until we fall asleep. Her house is amazing. She's amazing. Life is amazing.

Uh, I mean Viola's okaaay, I guess. She lets us watch a lot of TV. And I enjoy TV.

We're watching this show called *Knights Try, Buddy*. It's an epic love story about a prince and a princess, but the prince doesn't even know he's a prince!

Ooooh, coooool! Was he switched at birth?! Is there an evil fake prince taking his spot?! And trying to steal the princess?! And using the wrong fork for salad at dinner?!

Naw. He just got hit on the head and thinks he's a dragon.

Whoooa.

They're in love anyway. It's a really sweet story. Other than the parts where he tries to breathe fire on her.

bing bong!

Speaking of dragons, check out the book Bree is reading.

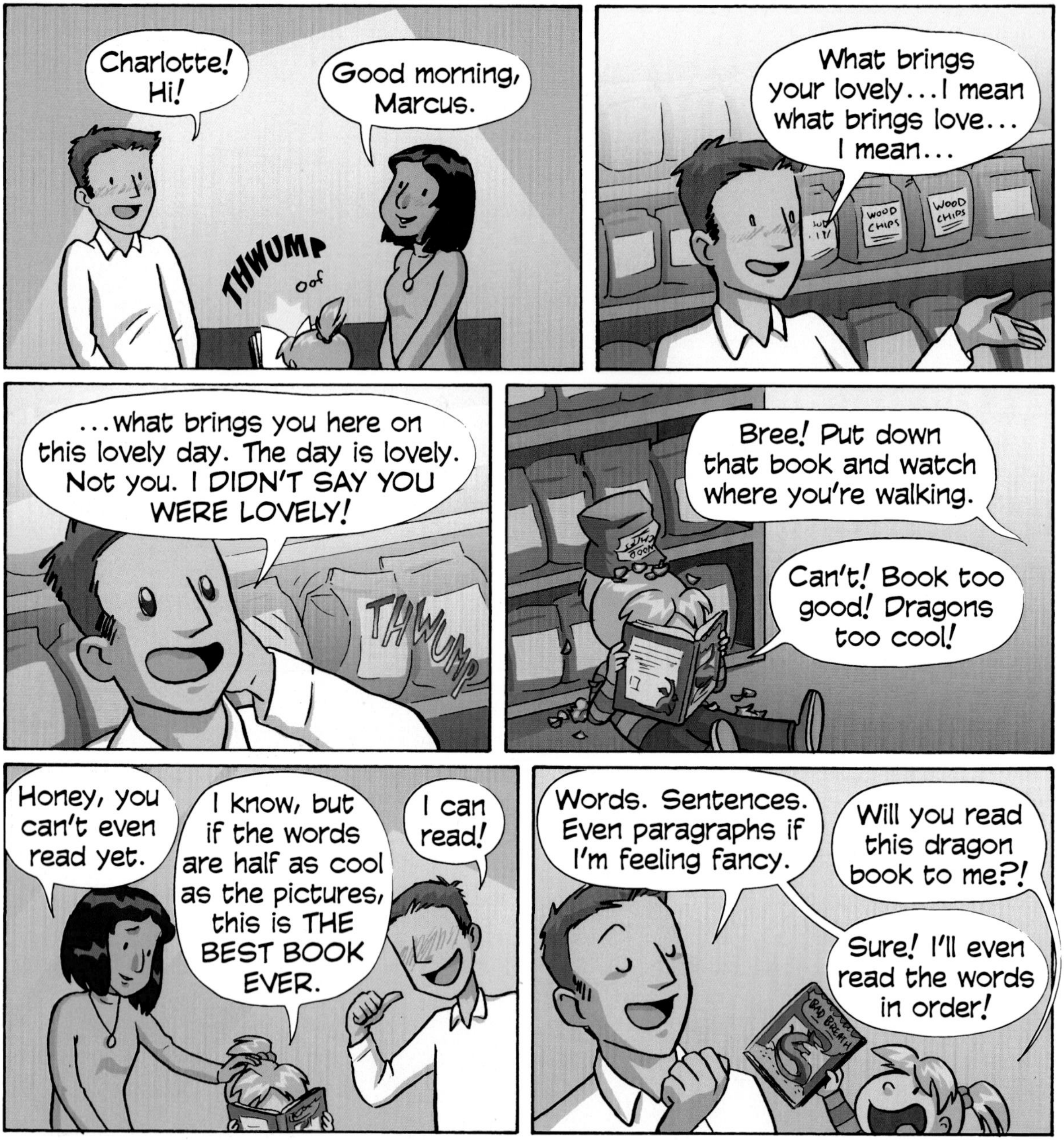
Charlotte! Hi!
Good morning, Marcus.
THWUMP
oof
What brings your lovely... I mean what brings love... I mean...
WOOD CHIPS
WOOD CHIPS
...what brings you here on this lovely day. The day is lovely. Not you. I DIDN'T SAY YOU WERE LOVELY!
THWUMP
Bree! Put down that book and watch where you're walking.
Can't! Book too good! Dragons too cool!
Honey, you can't even read yet.
I know, but if the words are half as cool as the pictures, this is THE BEST BOOK EVER.
I can read!
Words. Sentences. Even paragraphs if I'm feeling fancy.
Will you read this dragon book to me?!
Sure! I'll even read the words in order!
BAD BREATH

What about accountant?

Too boring.

Lion tamer?

Too dangerous.

How about 7 point 99?

That's just the price of the book.

Poo. That one sounded fun.

Look it's them!

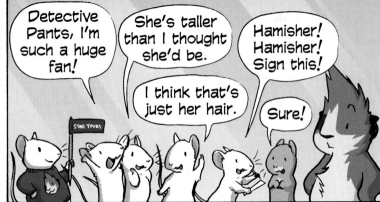

Detective Pants, I'm such a huge fan!

She's taller than I thought she'd be.

I think that's just her hair.

Hamisher! Hamisher! Sign this!

Sure!

Yield?

It's my favorite sign!

You know we aren't detectives anymore.

True, but you're even more famous now! All of the mice from the bakery love the plays that the hamsters do about your adventures.

Ugh. Those silly plays!

Thanks for the tour! Here are two free tickets to tonight's show. Enjoy!

Suuunflooower seeeeeeds.

All right, tourists! Time to go. Next stop: the legendary spot where a man once dropped an ENTIRE box of donuts and didn't notice.

Oooooooh!

Hey look! Over there! Mr. Venezi is talking to Charlotte!

SNAP

Don't look at me!

Sales are amazing, but we have more used-book donations then we have space for. We might have to...sigh. Never mind.

Are you doing OK since you stopped selling the pets?

Wonderful! Great! Is there a word better than "great"? Because that's what we are!

Hamisher! Did you just eat our tickets?!

Ummmm. Mmaay-ee?

We've even been getting fan mail!

Fan mail?

Fan mail?

I get one of these almost every day for the birds. People like their bills!

Oh, Marcus. That's not a fan letter, that's...

Um...what were you saying?

Huh? I was saying something?

Come on, Ham. Let's go get another book.

I'm gonna stay away from Gas-o Taco. Mr. V ate it, and now his face is all red! Charlotte, too!

I bet it's gas.

That's not gas. That's LOVE.

So exciting! What am I going to wear to the wedding?!

We'd better polish my helmet! Where'd it go?

I think Mr. Sparkles might be right.

Gas-o Taco makes you fall in love? Gross.

...but I never wanted eyebrows anyway, which brings me back to why I'm here. Have you seen Mr. V's pen? Snore once for yes, twice for no, three times if you think I should give eyebrows another chance...

The Amazing Adventures of Detective Pants and the other guy!

NEXT SHOW: when we wake up.

Interesting... seventeen snores. So you REALLY like eyebrows.

Hey, Detective Herbert.

The Other Guy?! Hmmph.

You know Mr. Venezi found his pen, right?

Mr. Venezi? Hmmm. The name sounds familiar...

I need to ask you some questions. It'll only take 30 seconds. Or maybe 50 seconds. Probably no more than 65 seconds. I've broken it down into eleven parts. Question one, part one...

Run, Hamisher! Run!

16

Wow. Charlotte wasn't kidding about having too many donations!

It looks like the whole place was trampled by a monster or some--

ROOOOAR!

Bree! Stop that. I just stacked those.

I'm not Bree anymore! I'm a dragon! Mr. V and I read all about them! They love gold and can breathe fire and don't like it when people touch their gold! Give me the gold! Give me the goooooldfish!

Bree, Mr. Venezi's not selling the pets anymore.

Sigh. I know. I just really wanted the goldfish.

Every dragon needs a good lair. Want to build one?

Let's collect all the gold color books.

YESSS.

You can come down now.

The view from up here is great! Wait, that's it! That's what we should be!

What? Mountain climbers? Explorers?

No. Taller!

I can't wait to move to the new bookstore! It's so huge we can make my dragon lair twice as big. Five times as big! Mr. V's going to be so excited! He can sleep in the mystery section!

Mr. Venezi won't be moving with us.

But we're only on page 16 in the dragon book!

I can't believe Charlotte is moving! She hasn't even told Mr. V yet! Where are we going to get our books? I'm so sad!

I'm sad too. We can order books online, but it's not the same. And I'm worried about our shop. I don't think Mr. V is paying the bills.

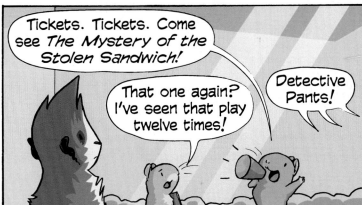

Tickets. Tickets. Come see *The Mystery of the Stolen Sandwich!*

That one again? I've seen that play twelve times!

Detective Pants!

You're my hero, Detective Pants!

You're so beautiful! What's your secret?

I work out.

I'm kind of glad you ate those tickets, Hamisher.

My, my. This town is going to have some stylish aardvarks!

AARDVARK neckties

♪BING BONG♪

Good morning! How many aardvarks do you have living in your walls?

I...I... hope I don't have any!

Shucks.

I just need some food for my precious Ruffles. He's very picky, so no dog food that tastes like dog food.

Have you considered getting Ruffles a perch? These flying things are called "birds," and they love them!

Ruffles is a very large DOG.

So you're saying you need a BIG perch...

Later that day...

How's it going, Mr. V?

Not great. I haven't sold a single toothbrush or necktie. All the walrus and aardvark owners must be going to another shop.

Sigh.

I have an idea! If the bookstore goes away, we can make our own books. That way the hamsters will have new stories to tell too!

Good thinking, Ham!

I'll write and I can teach you how to draw! First rule of drawing: always have something on your head!

Hmmm what to write about...what to write about? This is hard!

This is fun! I think I'm kinda good too.

Of course! You're good at everything you do!

Look, I painted you!

Awesooom...

...Um...did you keep your hat on the whole time?

bing bong

Oh! Mr. Westing.

Hi, Marcus.

You've always been one of my favorite tenants. But it's been months since you paid rent and...I have six grandkids to take care of and I...I can't keep waiting.

I can give you another week, but that's it. I'm sorry.

Mr. V, is everything okay?

Yeah, yeah. Just fine. Great. Is there a word better than great because that's what...

sigh

Are you sure? You're looking really dour.

Dour?

Gasp! That's it! I'll go dour-to-dour.

Do you mean door-to-door?

That's what I said. You're a genius, Viola!

22

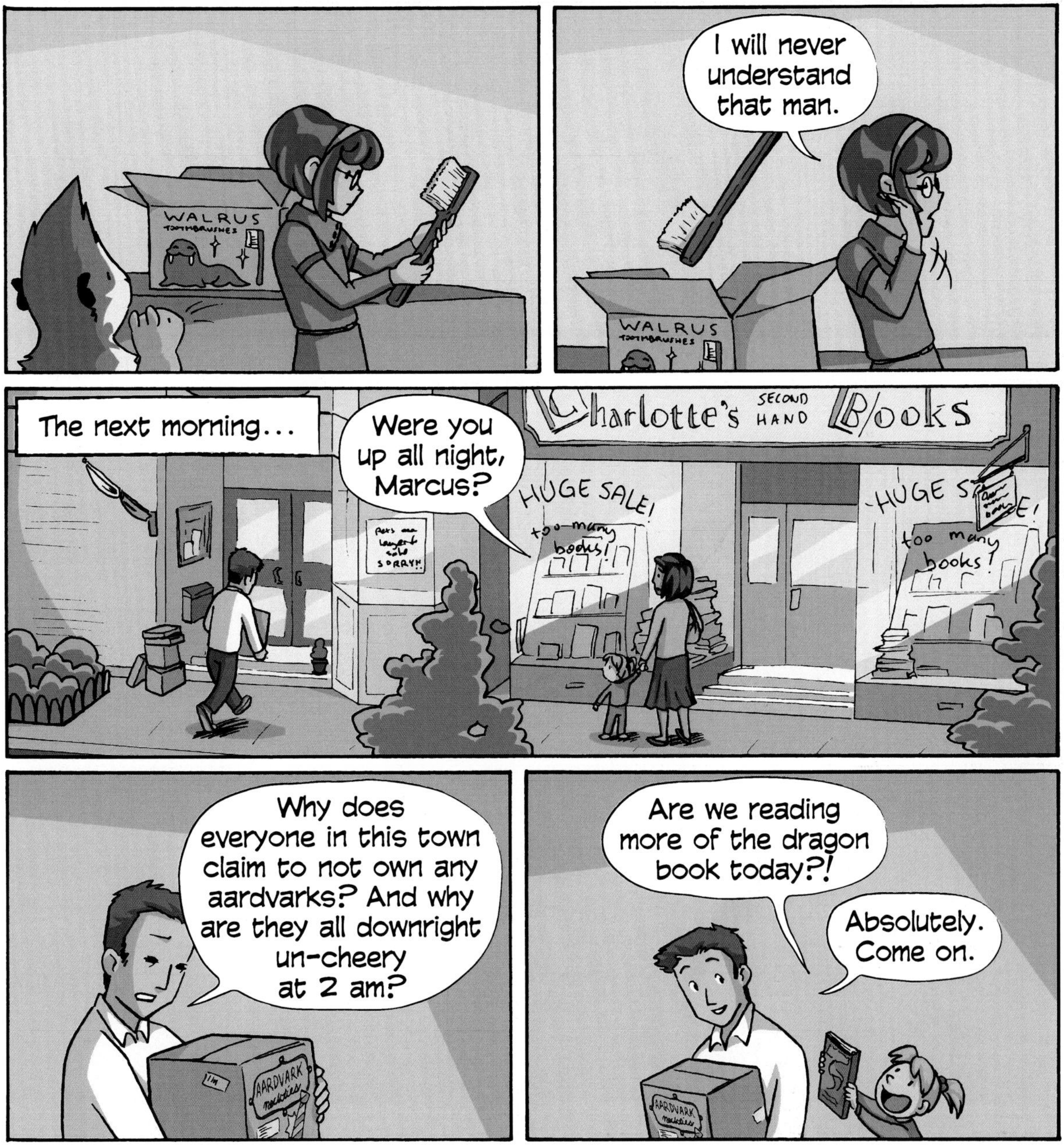
WALRUS
I will never understand that man.
The next morning...
Were you up all night, Marcus?
Charlotte's SECOND HAND Books
HUGE SALE!
too many books!
Why does everyone in this town claim to not own any aardvarks? And why are they all downright un-cheery at 2 am?
AARDVARK
Are we reading more of the dragon book today?!
Absolutely. Come on.

I'm just not sure what I'm going to do with all these-- walrus tooth...

We've been robbed!

Let's go over this one more time. What was stolen?

100 walrus toothbrushes and $1,000. Here's the $1,000.

If you HAVE the money, how can it be stolen?

It wasn't stolen from me. It was stolen from someone else. The walrus toothbrushes were mine though.

Not for my walruses. For other people's walruses.

Detective Herbert! There's a new case!

I don't know. I'm not that into fashion. And this shell-case makes me look handsome and curvy. Which reminds me...

You coming out of retirement yet, Detective Pants?

Nope, Gerry! Mr. V probably just forgot where he put those toothbrushes. I'm just glad he can pay rent now.

Hello, guinea pig. I'm only here because Mr. Sparkles made me carry him over to talk to you.

These boots aren't made for walking.

I wanted to give you a clue.

There's no mystery!

You're right, because Bree did it.

Wow. What a GOOD clue!

Did you see her do it?

No, but she's obsessed with dragons, and everyone knows dragons like to collect treasure and hide it.

It's gotta be her!

Gasp! Or what if it was a REAL dragon?!

Every good story has dragons...

How are you going to catch Bree? I mean, who knows who she took all that money from?

Bree's a good kid. If it WAS her, maybe she just found the money.

Yeah, Mr. Venezi is ALWAYS dropping things behind the counter.

Vioooola...

Sigh, did you lose ANOTHER shoe?

As long as Bree's not hurting anyone, it's fine. And I'm having fun making a book with Hamisher.

Gasp! That's what I can write about! The dragon!

Suit yourself, but I'd watch out. Even fake dragons can be dangerous.

OK! I'm ready. Aaaaand ACTION!

Um, Hamisher--

"The guinea pig hero raised her hand!"

"The guinea pig hero lowered her hand!"

"The guinea pig hero--"

Stop that!

You guys are so weird.

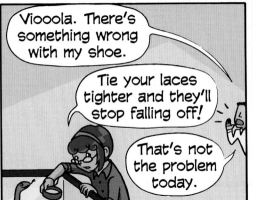
Viooola. There's something wrong with my shoe.

Tie your laces tighter and they'll stop falling off!

That's not the problem today.

RRRRROAARR!

BUMP!

Sorry. Bree's been a dragon lately.

I brought some breakfast donuts. Also, I need to tell you something.

A gift? For me?! That's so sweet. I, um, got you something too. It's right, uh...

Here?

Um. Thanks?

Whoa. What happened?

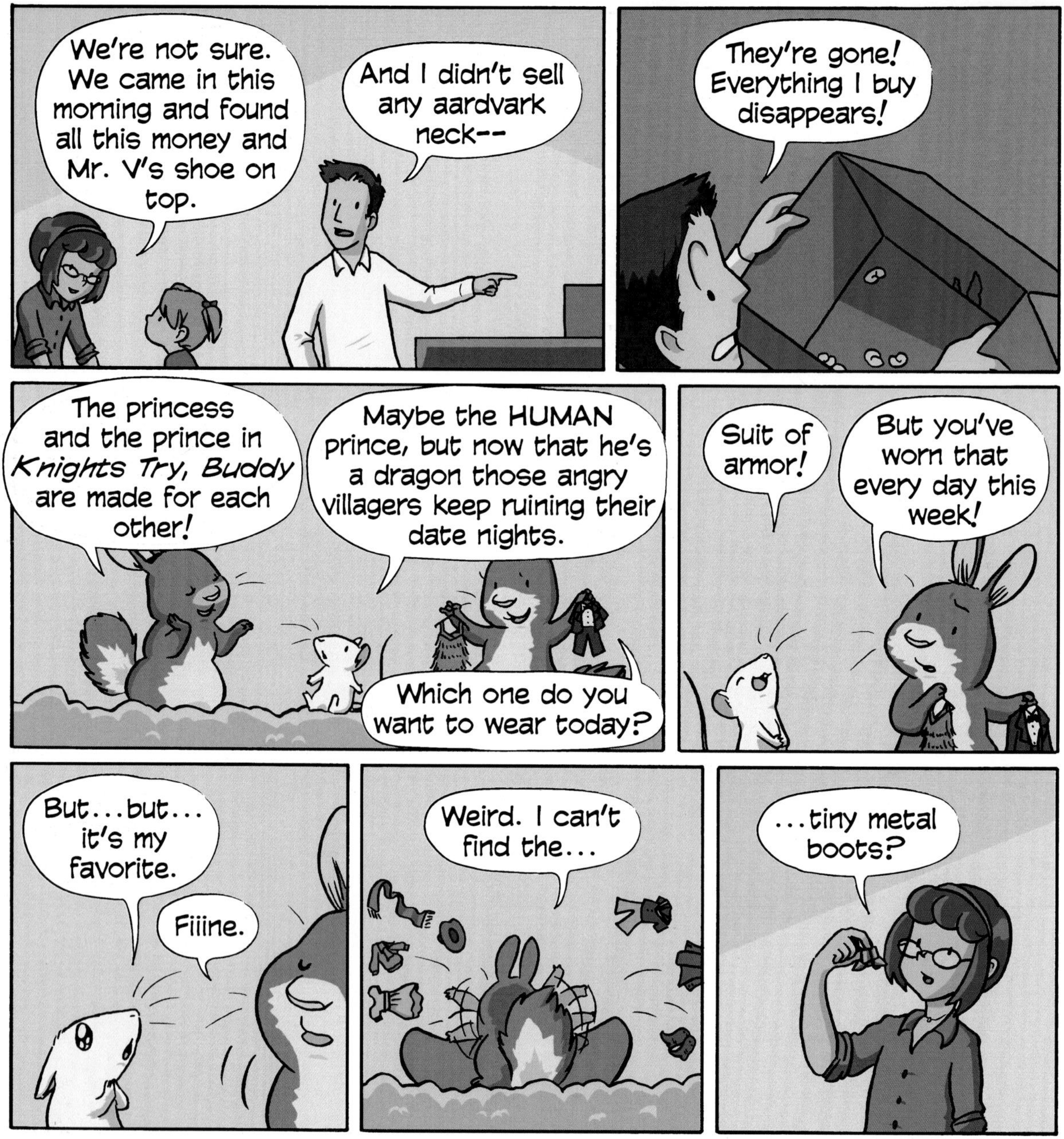
We're not sure. We came in this morning and found all this money and Mr. V's shoe on top.
And I didn't sell any aardvark neck--
They're gone! Everything I buy disappears!
The princess and the prince in *Knights Try, Buddy* are made for each other!
Maybe the HUMAN prince, but now that he's a dragon those angry villagers keep ruining their date nights.
Which one do you want to wear today?
Suit of armor!
But you've worn that every day this week!
But...but... it's my favorite.
Fiiine.
Weird. I can't find the...
...tiny metal boots?

How did these wind up in the register?

Knight's armor! The treasure! Your gold shoe! Gasp! Mr. V, you found a dragon den!!!

Don't touch anything! The dragon will get mad!

Bree, did you do this?

Nu-uh! My dragon den is next door!

And mine doesn't smell like feet.

Let's get this cleaned up.

Maybe we shouldn't touch anything.

Mr. V, there's no such thing as dragons!

Of course I know there's not. I don't believe in dragons. But if there WAS a dragon, it wears at LEAST three shoes! Maybe more!

Gulp!

A dragon?!

I know why I wasn't a great writer yesterday! In order to draw, I need something on my head. So in order to write, I need something on my foot!

I think I'm getting good at this! Look, I did a painting of Mr. Venezi.

Yeah, that's...really...uh...painty?

Detective Pants!

You've got to help!

Heeey, slow down, guys!

Whoa! Are you all mountain climbers now?

No. We're just scared!

There's a dragon in the shop!

We figured if we're tied together, we'll all be safe!

pant pant

You gotta help!

Guys, there isn't really a dragon. It's just...

Oh, man. This is good.

I think I pulled a butt muscle.

It was a dark and stormy night. The dragon lurked inside the walls of the pet shop.

His big scaly body hid in the shadows. Hungry. Waiting. Waiting...

I should work out.

...to STRIKE!

AAAAAAaaaaa AAAAHHHH!

I'll just stay here.

Not bad at all.

And I owe it all to my feet-hats! Thanks, feet-hats!

The villagers were terrified. Some tried to blend in.

If we look...

...like dragons...

...then the real dragon...

...will leave us alone!

Others hid.

NO RABBITS HERE

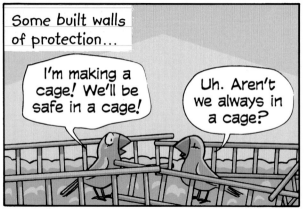

Some built walls of protection...

I'm making a cage! We'll be safe in a cage!

Uh. Aren't we always in a cage?

...and others put on eight pairs of pants, ten dresses, and fourteen hats!

Hmmm. I don't know, Ham. That line doesn't really make much sense in your story.

Yeah. You're right. Also, the numbers keep changing.

This is absurd!

Bree can't steal my clothes if I'm wearing them all!

He has a point, Clarisse.

My darling detective, don't you think this has gone on too long? Come out of retirement. Stop this craziness.

Hamisher is just having fun writing his story. No one is getting hurt.

Not true. I, for one, am hurt every time Herbert asks me about that missing pen. I can feel my brain cells popping.

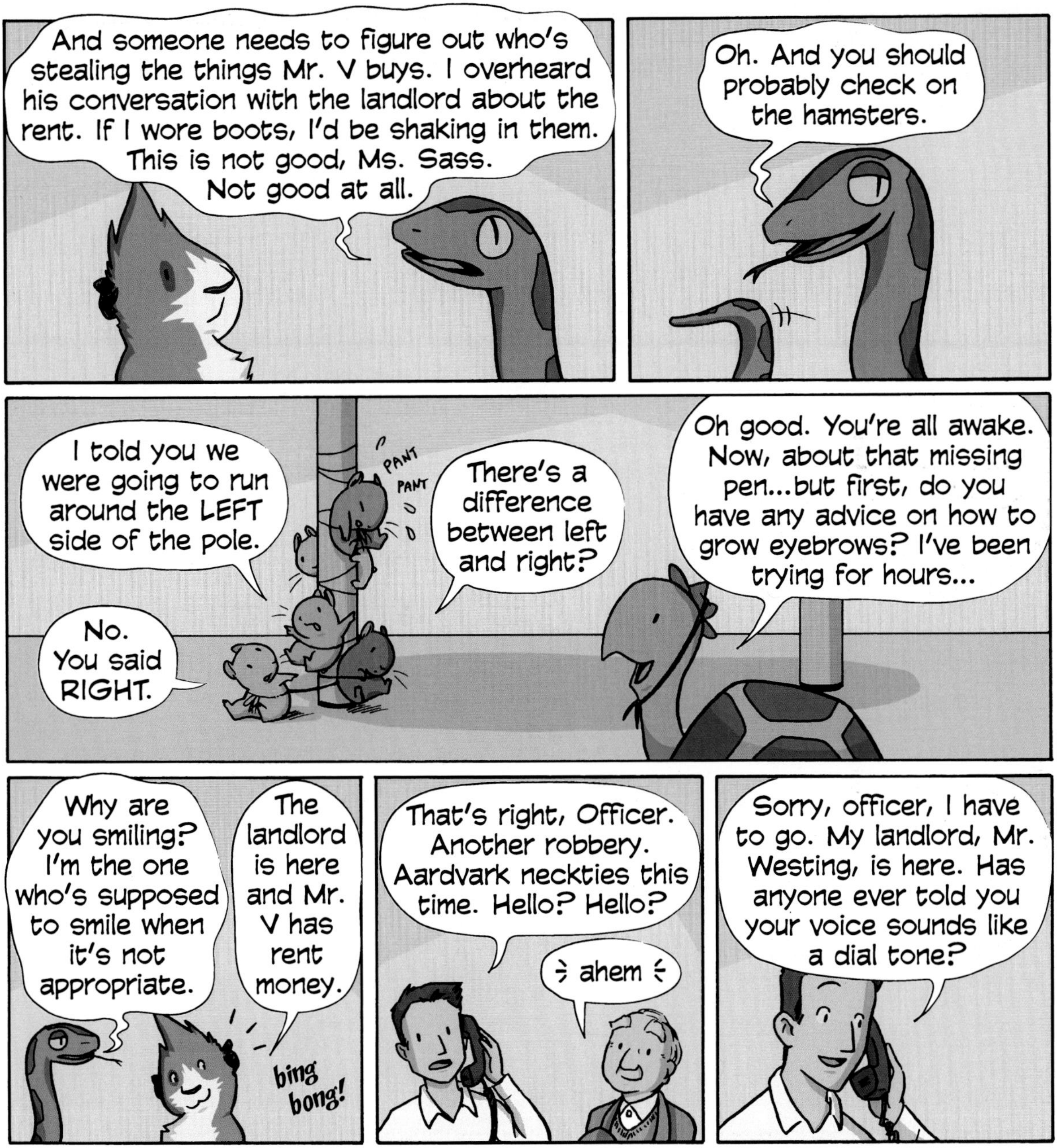
And someone needs to figure out who's stealing the things Mr. V buys. I overheard his conversation with the landlord about the rent. If I wore boots, I'd be shaking in them. This is not good, Ms. Sass. Not good at all.
Oh. And you should probably check on the hamsters.
I told you we were going to run around the LEFT side of the pole.
No. You said RIGHT.
PANT PANT
There's a difference between left and right?
Oh good. You're all awake. Now, about that missing pen...but first, do you have any advice on how to grow eyebrows? I've been trying for hours...
Why are you smiling? I'm the one who's supposed to smile when it's not appropriate.
The landlord is here and Mr. V has rent money.
bing bong!
That's right, Officer. Another robbery. Aardvark neckties this time. Hello? Hello?
ahem
Sorry, officer, I have to go. My landlord, Mr. Westing, is here. Has anyone ever told you your voice sounds like a dial tone?

The mail lady told me she's been picking up a lot of outgoing shipments from you lately. I was glad to hear that! I hope you earned enough to cover rent?

Shipments? What shipments?

I'm not sure what you're talking about, but I do have money. Loads of it! Actual piles!

You do?! Oh, thank goodness.

But it's part of a dragon's treasure, so I can't give it to you. Hey, I kept meaning to ask, does this building have a history of dragon infestation?

I'm sorry, Marcus. I really am. I thought this might be hard for you, so I made some calls. Mega Pet Mart has agreed to take all of your animals. They sell thousands of pets a day.

SIGH

Mega Pet Mart?

Take all of my animals?

Thousands?

I promised you a week. You still have two more days...I'll keep my fingers crossed.

No more playing around.

We have one more mystery ending to write!

YAY!

Theme music! Theme music! Theme music!

Theme music! Theme music! Theme music!

Theme music! Theme music! Theme music!

FLIP!

Theme music! Theme muuuuuuusic!

What are you singing?

Our theme song! I haven't figured out the words yet.

Okay. We need to get rid of the dragon, get Mr. V to use the money for rent, find a way to keep the shop open, and convince Charlotte not to move. Um...that should be...easy?

To the fish!

35

Thank goodness you're on the case!

Did you hear them talking about Mega Pet Mart?! You can't let that happen!

I can't feel my arms.

You have Viola. You won't get sent there.

I know, but...everyone should have a real home. Even guinea pig nerds deserve to be happy.

≥ cough ≤ Especially a guinea pig nerd who's helped me out so many times without me ever saying thank you. ≥ cough ≤

Awww.

Stop that! Now go and solve this case. You can't talk to the fish because Bree has been guarding them all day.

Guarding them?

So the "dragon" can't get their gold.

Don't worry, gold guys! I'm not gonna let the dragon lay a single dragon scale on you!

Scale?

I think the dragon's on a diet.

He did look a little fluffy...

If Bree is the dragon, why would she be worried about the fish?

The dragon must be someone else. My guess is the ferrets.

Ugh. It's so hard to take you seriously in that outfit... well in that MANY outfits.

You're breaking every fashion rule in the book!

The book...that gives me an idea!

The next morning...

Only two more mornings, turning this key. Then I'll have to lock up for good. Sigh.

Mr. V! Mr. V!

Hi. Can you come and look next door?

My books!

I knew it! The dragon's after the gold! I hope the fish are OK!

I'll help you carry the books back to your shop.

I thought you were afraid the dragon would get mad.

The dragon can do what it likes to my shoe, but I won't let it pick on you!

That's really sweet.

Even if we'll only be neighbors for a little while longer.

I don't want to move the bookstore, but I guess we have to.

Mr. Venezi's and Stuff is closing.

You're moving?!

You're closing?!

I'm really going to miss it here.

What if Mega Pet Mart puts us in a cage we can't fly out of?

They'll never find us, Molly.

We're practically ninjas, Martha.

NO RABBITS HERE

GO AWAY MEGA PET MART

Mega Pet Mart...

...doesn't sell

dragons.

We just have to get better...

...at breathing fire.

I hope this plan works.

I really hope so too, Ham.

bing bong

Hi, Mr. V! Hi, Charlotte!

Cool! A book mountain!

Awk! Polly want a cracker!

We need more food for Marcel.

Help yourself to bird food. Free of charge. I'm sad to say, but Mr. Venezi's and Stuff is closing.

Oh, this book looks good!

What? Why?! But we love your store!

Are you even listening?

Here's a dollar! Can I read to the rabbits, Mr. V?

Uh...I don't see why not...

Awesome! I can read and play with the animals at the same time!

How did they see us, Molly?

I'm not sure I care, Martha. This story is really good.

Here's the money for the book, Charlotte.

It's yours. You were the one who sold the book. Maybe it'll help you keep the shop open.

Without you next door, it doesn't seem to matter. Hey, do you think...maybe... Do you eat lunch?

I do eat lunch.

So do I!

Look at all this work! I should do all this work!

Don't worry. The dragon hasn't touched the goldfish. Why is everyone bright red? Did you guys get Gas-o Taco without me?!

I'll miss you, feet-hats, but I'm too sad to put you on again. I'm gonna miss being a detective. I'm gonna miss being a writer. I'm gonna miss being a dragon. I'm gonna miss my best friend...

Don't say good-bye to your feet-hats yet. The plan isn't over, but it's going to take everybody's help...

...especially the dragon.

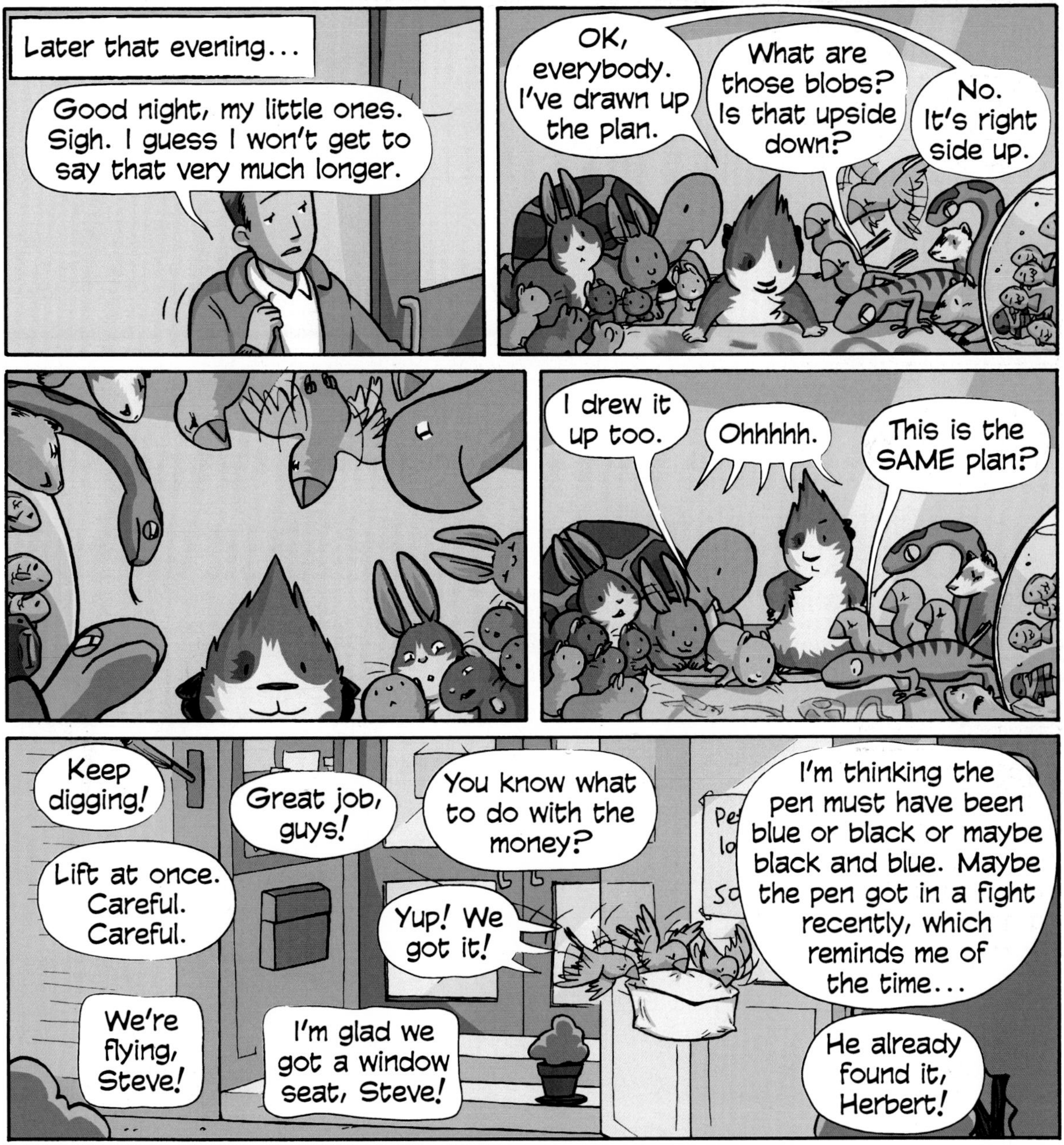
Later that evening...
Good night, my little ones. Sigh. I guess I won't get to say that very much longer.
OK, everybody. I've drawn up the plan.
What are those blobs? Is that upside down?
No. It's right side up.
I drew it up too.
Ohhhhh.
This is the SAME plan?
Keep digging!
Lift at once. Careful. Careful.
We're flying, Steve!
Great job, guys!
You know what to do with the money?
Yup! We got it!
I'm glad we got a window seat, Steve!
I'm thinking the pen must have been blue or black or maybe black and blue. Maybe the pen got in a fight recently, which reminds me of the time...
He already found it, Herbert!

That's odd.

Maybe Bree was right about the dragon wanting the goldfish.

Read me?

This is so exciting!

I've never been dragon treasure before.

Shhhh, I don't want to miss any of the movie.

Did anyone make popcorn?

To: Mr. V
From: The Dragon
READ ME!!!

A gift certificate for Amore Romantic Café? And what does this mean: "Ask her out"?

Briiiing

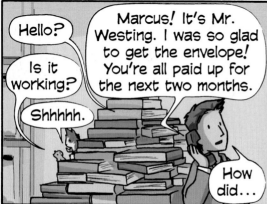

Hello?

Is it working?

Shhhhh.

Marcus! It's Mr. Westing. I was so glad to get the envelope! You're all paid up for the next two months.

How did...

I've moved so you don't have to. I gave Mr. Westing my treasure for RENT. It was nice living in Mr. Venezi's and Stuff. Bye! Heart, The Dragon
P.S. Did you ask her out yet?

Her?

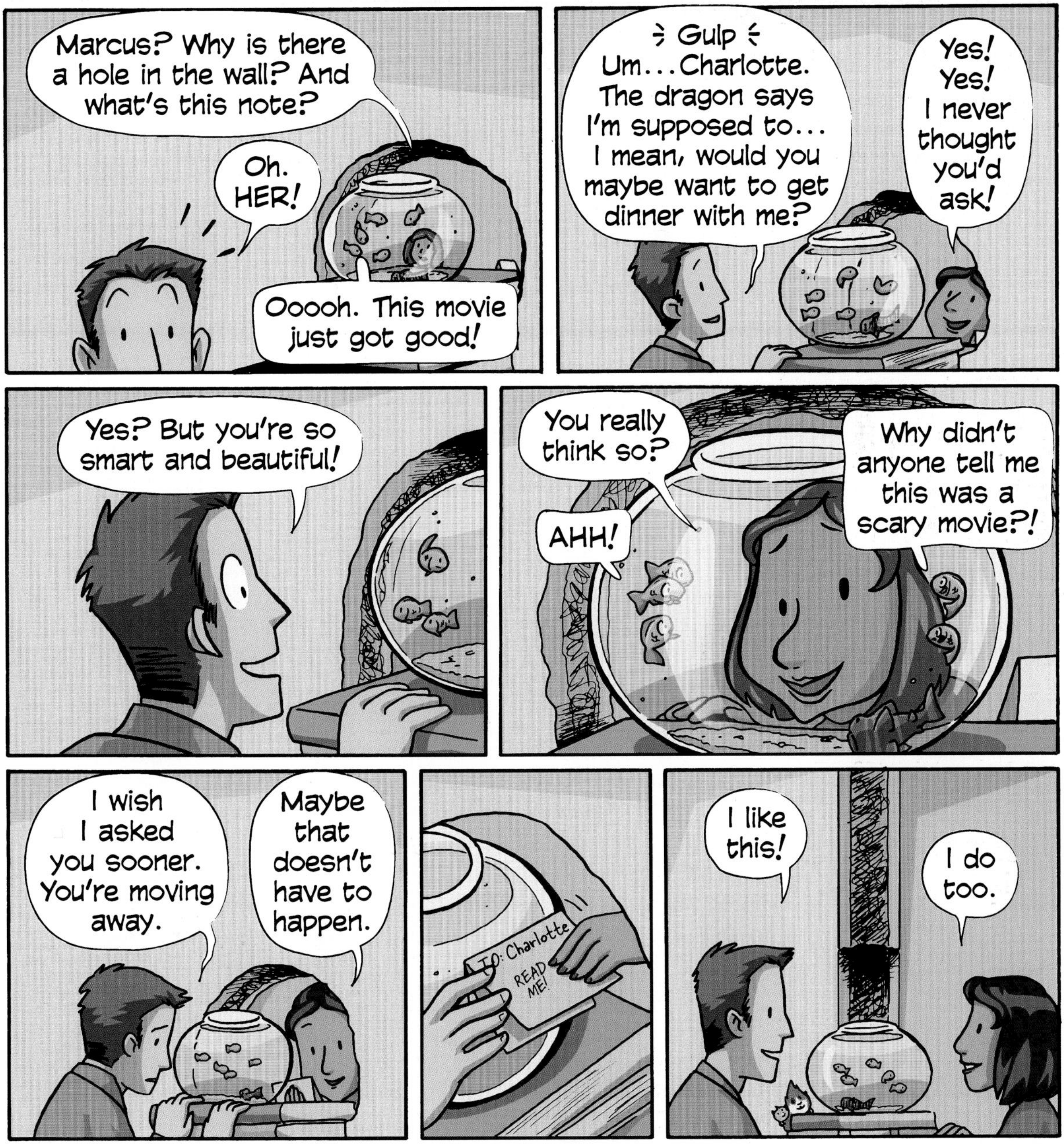

Marcus? Why is there a hole in the wall? And what's this note?
Oh. HER!
Ooooh. This movie just got good!
⋟ Gulp ⋞ Um... Charlotte. The dragon says I'm supposed to... I mean, would you maybe want to get dinner with me?
Yes! Yes! I never thought you'd ask!
Yes? But you're so smart and beautiful!
You really think so?
AHH!
Why didn't anyone tell me this was a scary movie?!
I wish I asked you sooner. You're moving away.
Maybe that doesn't have to happen.
TO: Charlotte
READ ME!
I like this!
I do too.

But what's that brown blob supposed to be?

I thought it was a really nice self-portrait, Sass.

Heeey.

Two months later...

Charlotte & Mr. Venezi's BOOKS & PETS & STUFF

44

Oh, great! The new sign is here.

I'll go put it up.

I wanna help!

And I'll get rid of these moving boxes!

bing bong

Did you hear? Tonight the hamsters are putting on a play I wrote! *The Unsolved Mystery of the Missing Aardvark Neckties and Also There Is a Dragon.* It's a pretty catchy title!

Do you think anyone will ever figure out it was us?

Naw.

Would you look at that...

ONLINE SALE:
TO: New York Aquarium
100 WALRUS TOOTHBRUSHES
SOLD BY: Mr. Venezi's A...
PAID $1,000

Wait a minute...the neckties went missing in the night everyone was watching the play other than Sasspants and Hamisher, and the fish described the dragon as "gray and fluffy and talks too much"... Which reminds me of the time...

I'm just glad we don't have to stay up all night selling walrus toothbrushes online or moving books so Mr. V would talk to Charlotte.

It gave me a lot to write about!

45

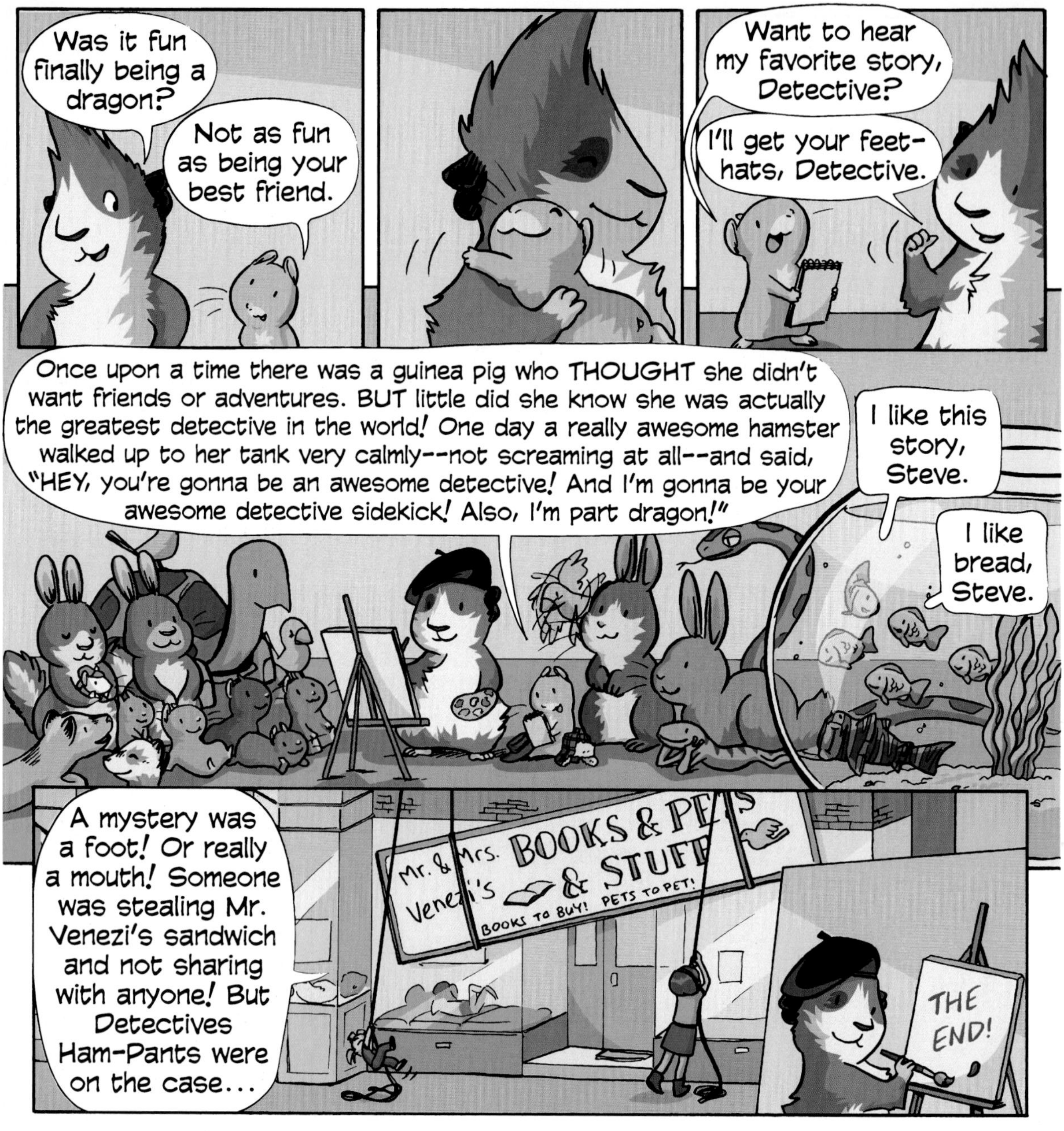
Was it fun finally being a dragon?
Not as fun as being your best friend.
Want to hear my favorite story, Detective?
I'll get your feet-hats, Detective.
Once upon a time there was a guinea pig who THOUGHT she didn't want friends or adventures. BUT little did she know she was actually the greatest detective in the world! One day a really awesome hamster walked up to her tank very calmly--not screaming at all--and said, "HEY, you're gonna be an awesome detective! And I'm gonna be your awesome detective sidekick! Also, I'm part dragon!"
I like this story, Steve.
I like bread, Steve.
A mystery was a foot! Or really a mouth! Someone was stealing Mr. Venezi's sandwich and not sharing with anyone! But Detectives Ham-Pants were on the case...
Mr. & Mrs. Venezi's BOOKS & PETS & STUFF
BOOKS TO BUY! PETS TO PET!
THE END!

HAMISHER EXPLAINS...

Guinea Pigs and Hamsters!

Look Sass! It's a section about us!

Sasspants was a natural detective because guinea pigs are really smart! They recognize people by scent or voice. They can even learn tricks. Guinea pigs are also one of the only animals who can see the same range of colors as humans. Dogs, cats, and even brainy dolphins can't see colors as well as guinea pigs!

Sasspants didn't think she wanted any friends, but she was happier once she made them. That's because in the wild guinea pigs always travel in herds. It's my scientific belief that a stampede of guinea pigs would be the cutest way to get trampled.

There are tons of different kinds of guinea pigs. Sometimes I make fun of Sasspants' hair, but it's not her fault. She's an Abyssinian, which is a type of guinea pig whose hair always looks like they slept on it funny. If you think her hair is silly, then you've never seen a Peruvian guinea pig. Their silky straight hair grows more than a foot long. It's like a wig with legs! There's even a guinea pig that has NO hair called a Skinny Pig. Some people mistake them for baby hippos.

I think Sasspants would make a GREAT president, but she wouldn't be the first guinea pig in the White House. Theodore Roosevelt had five guinea pigs with even crazier names than Detective Pants. He had Admiral Dewey and Fighting Bob Evans. Guinea pigs have even hung around with the queen! Queen Elizabeth I had one in the 1500s, and many say she's the reason they became popular. Rich ladies followed the queen's lead and kept guinea pigs, making their servants carry the guinea pigs around on fancy, schmancy silk pillows. Ooh la la!

Hamsters are NOT koalas. It was pretty hard to learn that but turns out we're pretty cool too! I'm a Roborovski dwarf hamster, which Sasspants tells me doesn't mean I'm part robot. Dam. Roborovskis are the smallest but also the speediest hamster. We can run faster than hamsters TWICE our size, up to 8 miles a night!

The name *hamster* comes from a German word meaning "to horde" or "to gather". We got that name because we can carry up to half our body weight in our cheek pouches! *Horde* is also the name for a group of us: a horde of hamsters. Try to say that three times fast with half your body weight in your mouth!

While we might not be carried around on silk pillows by rich people, we ARE Internet famous. One of the first websites to get millions of views was called the Hamster Dance! A student named Deidre LaCarte made the site for her hamster, Hampton. It was just four images of hamsters dancing to music. It was so popular that in three months over 17 million people watched it!

Thanks for reading about our adventures! And remember, you can totally be anything you want when you grow up! A detective, a writer, an artist, an ocean astronaut...well, maybe not a koala. It's really hard to be a koala when you grow up.

Meet the Writer and the Artist (and all their pets)!

Colleen, who writes the words:

Growing up, I had a dog named U.U., a cat named Kitty, a hermit crab named Herman, but more than anything, I wanted a hamster. My mother, who was originally from New York City, thought of anything tiny and fluffy as the enemy. "No rats in this house!," she'd say. So I decided that instead of an imaginary friend, I was going to have an imaginary hamster. His name was, you guessed it, Hamisher, and he imaginarily rode on my shoulder for a full year! The Guinea Pig books are basically a list of all the animals I wanted growing up: hamsters, guinea pigs, ferrets, and chinchillas, and Hamisher's personality was based on me as a kid: really, REALLY hyper. Sasspants, on the other hand, was inspired by my older sister, Kathleen, who was smart, tough, and would loooove it if her hyper younger sister left her alone. Best part of being an adult: You can have any pet you'd like! (Other than dragons. They are still illegal in most states...and also imaginary.) I've had many cool pets including a Roborovski dwarf hamster named Captain She-Hulk and four fish that are all 11 years old! The biggest is Emilio-The-Almost-An-Eel-io, who is a 13-inch-long bichir fish that looks a lot like a dinosaur. They are definitely less talkative than the goldfish in these stories but are often just as silly.

Colleen's advice for future writers!
The best way to become a better writer is to be a better reader. Like Sasspants, I read every day. It's fun, inspiring, and you'll learn a lot!

Stephanie, who draws the pictures:

My first real pet was a dwarf hamster bought from a seller in a street market in China, selling them from a bicycle basket. The hamster was creatively named Hamsterboy (it was meant as a nickname and stuck). Every day after school he would start stirring when I came home, waddle out to pee, have a bath, and then amble to the door of the birdcage, waiting for me to take him out to play. I owned a number of small pets since then—a pair of mice in college (Pandora and Gadget), a couple of rats (Skull and Bones), and a hamster duo (Mike and Joel) that unexpectedly gave birth to more hamsters. We found homes for most of the babies, but the one we called TV's Frank, the hamster Hamisher is based on, stayed with me. Currently, I have one Chinese dwarf hamster roommate, Wicket (no relation to Hamsterboy, the dwarf hamster from China). He likes grapes and working out.

Stephanie's advice for future artists!
Keep drawing, like Hamisher! Always draw. Draw from life, draw the things around you, and keep your sketchbooks close by!